YOU
NEVER
CAN
TELL

YOU NEVER CAN TELL

Adapted & Illustrated
by JANICE HOLLAND
From the translation by
ARTHUR W. HUMMEL
from
The Book of HUAI NAN TZU
written before 122 B.C.

CHARLES SCRIBNER'S SONS · NEW YORK

Printed in the United States of America

Library of Congress Catalog Card Number 61-13374

NOTE:

This is a tale which the storytellers of China have told on fair days and market days for hundreds of years.

Indeed, THE GREAT WALL, which the peaceful Chinese built along fourteen hundred miles of wild frontier, was new when this story was first written down.

Long ago in China, when all the land was fair and green, there lived an old man and his wife.

Their life was simple, and above all else they loved three things: their son, their horse, and their farm.

They loved their son for reasons that everyone knows. They loved their horse because he was strong and pulled their plow.

They loved their farm, for in its yellow earth grew all the food that gave them life.

The son was named Liang. The horse was named Chih-tu. But the farm was so small that it had no name at all.

One day, for reasons which no one knows, their horse wandered away.

The farmer and his son, Liang, looked by the white waters that foamed in the brook. But the horse, Chih-tu, was not there.

Together the farmer and his son searched the road to the Jade Pagoda. But their horse was nowhere to be seen.

Dusty and tired, they started for home.

By this time the farmer's wife had told all the neighbors that the horse, Chih-tu, was lost. So when the farmer and his son drew near the house, they heard a great sound of wailing and weeping, for every neighbor had also a horse which he loved, and the loss of one horse struck terror into the hearts of all.

The oldest man in the village stroked his beard. "Your horse has no doubt wandered beyond the Great Wall into no-man's-land," he croaked.

"The fierce horsemen who live there must have stolen him by now!" said the schoolmaster.

"Never again will you see that horse," said the maker of shoes. "Sorrow and sadness. Woe and weeping. Ill luck indeed has come to this house!" wailed all the neighbors together.

Now all this while the farmer stood by the door, listening and watching, but never saying a word.

"Come now," said the maker of shoes. "We are all here to join you in sorrow. But you do not seem sad. Is it possible that you

do not mind losing your horse? Without your horse you cannot plow your farm. Without plowing your farm you cannot grow your food. Without any food you will certainly starve!"

But the old farmer only shook his head and said, "You never can tell. This may turn out to be a good thing after all. You never can tell," he said. "You never can tell."

Day after day the farmer searched the road to the Jade Pagoda.

Day after day his son looked through the woods beside the foaming brook.

But the horse, Chih-tu, was gone.

The mid-autumn festival came and went. One moon followed another across the sky.

The old farmer sighed to himself. "Alas for Chih-tu. Alas."

And after that he searched no more.

Now it was early in the year, and the willow trees were pale, pale green. One morning the old farmer awoke long before dawn.

Thrump-de-dump! Thrump-de-dump!

The farmer sat straight up in bed.

Thrump-de-dump! Thrump-de-dump! Louder and louder grew the noise.

Quickly the farmer jumped out of his bed.

Quickly he hurried through the courtyard to the gate in the wall.

Just beyond the gate he could dimly see something moving. "Chih-tu!" he called. "Chih-tu!" Soon a soft velvet nose was thrust through the gate.

Chih-tu had come home!

The old farmer opened the gate, and Chih-tu trotted in, for all the world as though he had never been away.

Before the old man could close the gate, a strange black horse had followed Chih-tu into the courtyard.

The farmer stared. The strange horse was the most beautiful horse he had ever seen.

"Now where in this world did you come from?" he asked, half under his breath.

But the strange horse, of course, answered never a word.

Now the farmer knew all his neighbors for miles around, and their horses as well. So he went at dawn to the highway, and asked of all passers-by where the fine steed might belong.

But no one knew.

It was just as though the black horse had dropped from the sky.

Before many hours had passed the farmer's wife again told all the villagers the news.

"Just to think," she cackled in her high-pitched voice, "today we have two horses, whereas yesterday we had none at all!"

Now the villagers, always eager for a good time, crowded once more into the farmer's house.

"Heaven has smiled on this house today!" they shouted all together. "Gladness and joy. Good fortune and blessings. Heaven has smiled on this house today!"

But the old farmer only stood by the door, listening and watching, but never saying a word.

"Come now," said the schoolmaster. "We are here to make merry. Can it be that you do not rejoice in your luck?"

But the old farmer only smiled and said, "How do we know that this is such a good thing after all? You never can tell," he said. "You never can tell."

Happy were the days that followed for the farmer and his family!
The red Chih-tu and the strange black horse worked together
to plow the little farm.

Soon the yellow earth was ready for the planting. Soon the
farmer's wheat was green above the ground. So well did every-
thing grow that the farmer's son, Liang, had plenty of time to
do as he liked.

Day after day Liang mounted one horse or the other and rode
around the farm.

Day after day Liang practiced one clever stunt or another until his riding was the envy of all the villagers. At last he became so daring that there was no risk he would not take.

As one might have expected, it was not long before he fell from his horse and broke a leg.

By this time it was late summer, and the wheat was ready for the harvesting.

"Ah, weeping and woe!" cried the neighbors when they heard of the fall. "How will the old man harvest his wheat without the help of his son?"

Once more they flocked into the farmer's courtyard to comfort him in his trouble.

"Sorrow and sadness. Weeping and woe! Ill luck indeed has come to this house!" wailed all the neighbors together.

Now all this while the farmer stood by the door, listening and watching, but never saying a word.

"Come now," said the oldest man in the village. "We are all here to join you in sorrow. But you do not seem sad. Is it possible you do not mind that your son has broken his leg?"

But the old farmer only smiled and shook his head. "You never can tell. This may turn out to be a good thing after all. You never can tell," he said. "You never can tell."

Strange to say, soon after this the fierce horsemen broke through the Great Wall.

Down they came, like thunder, across the farms and fields. "Ai-yah!" they shrieked. "Ai-yah!"

They rode into the villages and broke through the gates and doors.

Each strong young man they could find was seized and bound, for the wild tribes were hard pressed in a desert war. They needed men to help them fight.

So many wild riders there were that the strongest youth could not resist them. Nine out of ten young men were seized and bound.

Swiftly the riders had come, and swiftly they now departed. Slowly the dust settled back into the lanes and courtyards. Among many families, only the old farmer's was safe from harm.

Because the father was old, and the son was still lame, the wild tribes had passed them by.

The neighbors soon came to see the old farmer. Sad they were, for their grief was still fresh. As they looked at his son they remembered their own brave sons who were gone.

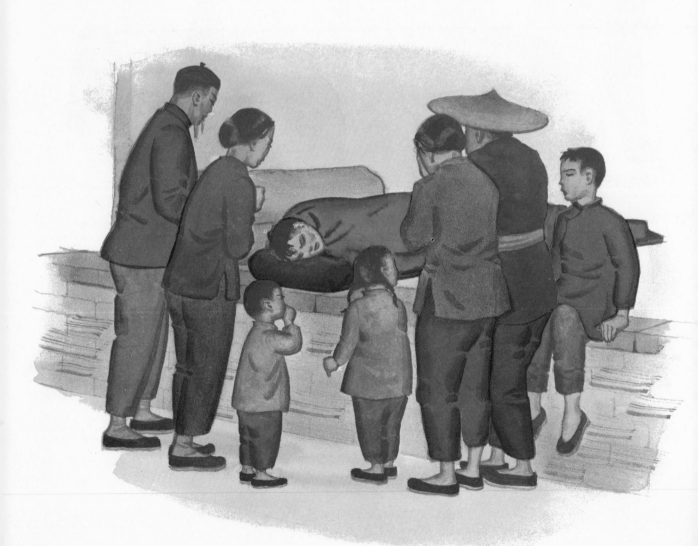

Then the oldest man in the village spoke: "Strange are the ways of fate. The wild tribes came in my youth. Many of us were carried away, but many at last returned. Some gathered riches before they came home. Some went to the cities and rose to great power.

"So, here today, we shall not weep, for we have seen that the sorrows sometimes bring their blessings. Nor yet can our hearts make merry, for we have seen that the joys many times bring their sorrows. As for which is the good, and which is the bad, you have spoken most truly, 'You never can tell.'"

"He has spoken most truly, most truly indeed," said all the neighbors together.

"For you never can tell," they said. "You never can tell."

"Yes," agreed the old farmer. "That one thing is true. You never can tell," he said. "You never can tell."

An ancient Chinese tale, adapted and illustrated, proves the wisdom of a poor farmer's conviction.